FARMINGTON COMMUNITY LIBRARY
FARMINGTON BRANCH LIBRARY
23500 LIBERTY STREET
FARMINGTON, MI 48335-3570
(248) 553-0321

FARMINGTON COMMUNITY LIBRARY

3 0036 01333 8015

Parents and Caregivers

Stone Arch Readers are designed to provide enjoyable reading experiences, as well as opportunities to develop vocabulary, literacy skills, and comprehension. Here are a few ways to support your beginning reader:

- Talk with your child about the ideas addressed in the story.

- Discuss each illustration, mentioning the characters, where they are, and what they are doing.

- Read with expression, pointing to each word. You may want to read the whole story through and then revisit parts of the story to ensure that the meanings of words or phrases are understood.

- Talk about why the character did what he or she did and what your child would do in that situation.

- Help your child connect with characters and events in the story.

Remember, reading with your child should be fun, not forced. Each moment spent reading with your child is a priceless investment in his or her literacy life.

Gail Saunders-Smith, Ph.D.

S0-AYO-343

DEC 0 4 2019

STONE ARCH READERS

are published by Stone Arch Books
A Capstone Imprint
1710 Roe Crest Drive
North Mankato, Minnesota 56003
www.capstonepub.com

Copyright © 2013 by Stone Arch Books
All rights reserved. No part of this publication may be reproduced in whole
or in part, or stored in a retrieval system, or transmitted in any form or by
any means, electronic, mechanical, photocopying, recording, or otherwise,
without written permission of the publisher.

Library of Congress Cataloging-in-Publication Data
 Meister, Cari.
 The grumpy lobster / by Cari Meister; illustrated by Steve Harpster.
 p. cm. — (Stone Arch readers—ocean tales)
 Summary: Arno the lobster is always grumpy and his friends are starting to
avoid him—can he change or will he always be alone?
 ISBN 978-1-4342-4025-5 (library binding) — ISBN 978-1-4342-4230-3 (pbk.)
 1. Lobsters—Juvenile fiction. 2. Mood (Psychology)—Juvenile fiction. 3.
Friendship—Juvenile fiction. [1. Lobsters—Fiction. 2. Mood (Psychology)—Fiction.
3. Friendship—Fiction.] I. Harpster, Steve, ill. II. Title.
PZ7.M515916Gru 2012
[E]—dc23

                    2011050082

            Art Director: Kay Fraser
            Designer: Russell Griesmer
        Production Specialist: Kathy McColley

            Reading Consultants:

          Gail Saunders-Smith, Ph.D.
          Melinda Melton Crow, M.Ed.
        Laurie K. Holland, Media Specialist

      Printed in the United States of America.
          122018   001318

3 0036 01333 8015

The Grumpy LOBSTER

by Cari Meister
illustrated by Steve Harpster

STONE ARCH BOOKS
a capstone imprint

LOBSTER FUN FACTS

- Lobsters come in lots of colors, including blue, yellow, greenish-brown, and gray. But no matter what color they are, they turn red when cooked.

- Lobster blood is clear.

- If a lobster loses a leg, claw, or an antenna, it can grow a new one.

- Today, lobster is considered a fancy food. But in Colonial times, it was a poor-quality food served only to children, servants, and prisoners.

Arno was always grumpy. He was grumpy when he woke up.

"Squid for breakfast again?" he said. "Yuck."

Arno was grumpy at school.

"Same dull stuff," he said.
"When will we learn something
interesting?"

Arno was even grumpy at his own birthday party.

"Another year older. Why
should I celebrate?" he asked.

At the spelling bee, Arno won
first place. But even that didn't
make him happy.

"Good job!" said his teacher.
"Here is your prize."

"A shell?" asked Arno. "A shell is my prize?"

He snapped his claw in disgust. "You should give better prizes," he said.

Arno's friends tried to make him feel better.

"Cheer up," said Niki the crab. "It's a great day!"

"What's so great about it?" Arno replied.

"Try to look on the bright side," said Lars the clam.

"There is no bright side," Arno answered. "We live on the dark ocean floor."

After a while, no one wanted
to be around Arno.

"All you do is complain," said
Niki.

"No one wants to be around
a grump," said Lars.

Arno swished his fan-like tail
and pushed himself backward.

"Fine! I don't need any friends!" said Arno. He hid in a cave.

While he hid in the cave, Arno could hear his friends having a great time.

They raced and played games.
They went midnight hunting.

No one missed Arno or his
grumpiness.

After a few hours, Arno was lonely. He wanted his friends back.

"Nobody likes me," he said.

A starfish heard him.

"Why not?" asked the starfish.

"They say I'm a grump," said Arno.

"Well," said the starfish, "are you?"

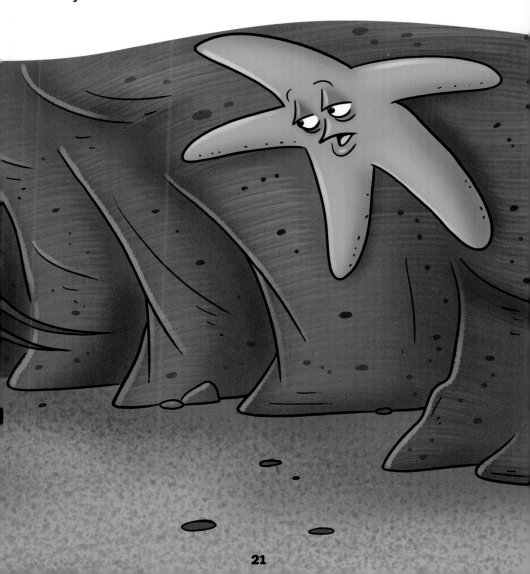

But before Arno answered,
the starfish scooted off. Arno
was alone again.

Arno poked out of his hole. He slowly climbed out of the cave.

Arno stuck his legs into the sand and sighed. He knew the answer to the starfish's question.

"Yes!" he said. "I've been a grump. A big snapping grump! But not anymore!"

Then he smiled. "If I want my friends back, I need to change my attitude," he said.

Arno called to his friends. "What are you playing?" he asked.

"Catch!" said Niki.

"Can I play?" asked Arno.

"Are you sure you want to play?" asked Niki.

"Yes," said Arno. "I'm sorry I've been such a grump!"

Arno played with his friends
for the rest of the day. They all
had a great time.

"Thanks, guys!" said Arno.
"This was the best day ever!"

The next morning, Arno
woke up grumpy. He was about
to complain about breakfast.
But then he remembered the
starfish.

"Squid!" he said. "Sounds tasty!"

The End

STORY WORDS

grumpy

squid

interesting

celebrate

disgust

complain

midnight

attitude

Total Word Count: 430

WHO ELSE IS SWIMMING IN THE OCEAN?

✓ S0-AZK-127

3 4028 06306 1361
HARRIS COUNTY PUBLIC LIBRARY

J 741.597 Tel
Telgemeier, Raina
The truth about Stacey : a
 graphic novel

                              $16.99
                        ocm71814647
1st ed.   07/23/2007

WITHDRAWN

Ann M. Martin

The BABY-SITTERS CLUB

The Truth About Stacey

A GRAPHIC NOVEL BY
RAINA TELGEMEIER

graphix

AN IMPRINT OF

SCHOLASTIC

NEW YORK TORONTO LONDON AUCKLAND SYDNEY MEXICO CITY NEW DELHI HONG KONG BUENOS AIRES

Kristy Thomas
President

Claudia Kishi
Vice-President

Mary Anne Spier
Secretary

Stacey McGill
Treasurer

Chapter 2

A FEW MINUTES LATER...

THE OTHER BABY-SITTERS ARE OLDER THAN WE ARE. THEY CAN STAY OUT LATER....

WHO **ARE** LIZ LEWIS AND MICHELLE PATTERSON?

THE FLIER SAYS THE BABY-SITTERS ARE "THIRTEEN AND OLDER." LIZ AND MICHELLE PROBABLY GO TO THE HIGH SCHOOL.... I WONDER IF MY BROTHERS KNOW THEM?

NO, THEY GO TO STONEYBROOK MIDDLE SCHOOL. THEY'RE EIGHTH GRADERS.

RRRIP

ARE YOU FRIENDS WITH THEM, CLAUD?

I'D NEVER BE FRIENDS WITH GIRLS LIKE THEM. LIFESAVER?

UM, MY DIABETES? I CAN'T HAVE ONE.

OH, YEAH. SORRY, STACEY. --KRISTY?

IT'S OKAY.

SO WHAT'S WRONG WITH THEM?

THEY HAVE SMART MOUTHS, THEY SASS THE TEACHERS, THEY HANG AROUND AT THE MALL. Y'KNOW, **THAT** KIND OF KID.

IT DOESN'T MEAN THEY'RE NOT GOOD BABY-SITTERS....

I'D BE SURPRISED IF THEY WERE.

I WONDER HOW THE AGENCY WORKS. THERE'S ONLY TWO NAMES ON THIS FLIER, BUT IT SAYS YOU CAN GET IN TOUCH WITH A "WHOLE NETWORK OF RESPONSIBLE BABY-SITTERS."

RING... RING...

HI, LIZ?

MY NAME IS, UH, CANDY. CANDY KANE... NO, NO JOKE...

I GOT YOUR FLIER FOR THE BABY-SITTERS AGENCY. I'M SUPPOSED TO SIT FOR MY LITTLE BROTHER TOMORROW, AND... UM...

UH, I JUST GOT ASKED OUT ON A DATE.

giggle

FROM 3:00 TO 5:00. HE'S SEVEN YEARS OLD. WILL **YOU** BE SITTING FOR HIM? UH-HUH... OH, I SEE.

hee hee hee

mmmfff!!!

I'LL BE AT 555-2321. OH, BUT ONLY FOR ABOUT TEN MORE MINUTES. THEN I HAVE... I HAVE ANOTHER DATE.... WHO WITH?

DON'T **DO** THAT WHEN I'M ON THE **PHONE!**

HA HA HEH...

BUT WINSTON **CHURCHILL?!** THE HIGH SCHOOL GUY YOU'RE **DATING?!**

OKAY, OKAY... I THINK THIS IS HOW THE AGENCY WORKS.

LIZ AND MICHELLE TAKE CALLS FROM CLIENTS, THEN SIMPLY TURN AROUND AND **FIND** THE SITTERS.

NO WONDER THEIR SITTERS ARE SO OLD. ALL LIZ AND MICHELLE HAVE TO DO IS CALL UP OLDER KIDS.

YEAH. WE COULD HAVE THOUGHT OF THAT, I GUESS.

LIZ SEEMED MORE INTERESTED IN MY "DATE" THAN IN FINDING A BABY-SITTER.

RING!

HELLO, THE BABY-SI-- ... HELLO?

YES, GREAT. **HOW** MANY? ... WOW. HOW OLD ARE THEY? ... WOW. OKAY. ... PATRICIA? SURE, THANKS. I'LL SEE PATRICIA TOMORROW AT THREE. ... LATER.

STACEY'S DINNER PLATE:

APPLE-GLAZED PORK CHOP
CALORIES: 194
CARBOHYDRATES: 4.8G
EXCHANGE: 1/4 BREAD/STARCH, 1 MEAT

STEAMED DILL CARROTS
(YUCK)
CALORIES: 31
CARBOHYDRATES: 3G
EXCHANGE: 1 VEGETABLE

ROMAINE LETTUCE SALAD
WITH LOW-CAL ITALIAN DRESSING
CALORIES: 39
CARBOHYDRATES: 2.8G
EXCHANGE: 1 VEGETABLE

Chapter 3

LATER THAT EVENING...

HONEY, ARE YOU FEELING ALL RIGHT? YOU HAVEN'T EATEN MUCH DINNER.

I'M NOT VERY HUNGRY.

ARE YOUR BLOOD SUGARS RUNNING HIGH?

I WAS 105 BEFORE DINNER, OK?

DO YOU THINK I **WANT** TO MAKE MYSELF GET SICK?

NO...I'M SORRY, HONEY. IT'S JUST THAT...

YOU'VE LOST THREE POUNDS THIS MONTH, AND... ARE YOU **SURE** YOU'RE FEELING ALL RIGHT?

YES. MAYBE I'M MORE ACTIVE NOW THAT I HAVE SOME FRIENDS HERE. MAYBE I NEED TO EAT **MORE**.

BUT YOU JUST SAID YOU WEREN'T HUNGRY. I'LL CALL THE DOCTOR ON MONDAY.

JUST IN CASE.

OH, YEAH! IN NEW YORK, I HAD THIS FRIEND NAMED LAINE.

I LOVED GOING TO HER APARTMENT, BECAUSE HER MOM WOULD BUY MILKY WAY BARS AND KEEP THEM IN THE FREEZER.

BITING INTO ONE OF THOSE WAS LIKE BITING INTO A FROZEN CHOCOLATE MILKSHA--

UM . . .

WELL, THIS WAS **BEFORE** I GOT SICK. ANYWAY, I KNOW WHAT YOU MEAN.

YEAH!

KRISTY, THIS IS GETTING OUT OF HAND. THE KID-KIT IS A GOOD IDEA, BUT LOWER RATES? HOUSEWORK? GIVING AWAY OUR JOBS?

NO, NO, NO. IF THAT'S WHAT THIS CLUB IS GOING TO BECOME, THEN I DON'T WANT TO BE IN IT.

ME NEITHER.

YOU GUYS, I DON'T WANT THE CLUB TO FALL APART. WE **CAN'T** LET LIZ AND MICHELLE BEAT US.

I THINK WE SHOULD USE TWO OF KRISTY'S IDEAS: THE KID-KITS AND THE SPECIAL DEALS.

BUT WE SHOULD SAVE THE OTHER IDEAS AS LAST RESORTS.

THAT'S FOR SURE.

WELL, WE CAN AT LEAST START MAKING THE KID-KITS. CLAUD, DO YOU HAVE ANY EMPTY BOXES?

OH, YEAH! LET ME GO GRAB SOME FROM THE BASEMENT.

WAIT RIGHT HERE.

I HAVE GLITTER, AND FABRIC, AND PAINTS, AND ALL SORTS OF THINGS WE CAN DECORATE THEM WITH!

COOL!

TUG

ART SUPPLI

THESE WILL BE THE BEST BOXES EVER!!

KID K

November 10

   Monday I had a sitting job for Charlotte Johanssen. I
love sitting for Charlotte, she's one of my very favorite kids.
And her mother, Dr. Johanssen, is a Doctor at Stoneybrook
Medical Center, so I like talking to her — she always asks me
how I'm doing and how I feel about my treatments. Today
was no different, except for what happened near the end
of the afternoon...

   Stacey

37

MY BEST FRIEND. WELL, SHE **USED** TO BE MY BEST FRIEND.

WHY DID SHE TEASE YOU?

IT'S A LONG STORY.

YOU DON'T WANT TO TALK ABOUT IT EITHER?

I GUESS NOT.

LOOK AT **THAT!!**

HI!

40

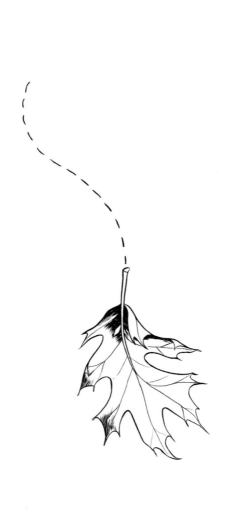

Sunday, November 23

It is just one week since Liz Lewis and Michelle Patterson sent around their fliers. Usually, our club gets about fourteen or fifteen jobs a week. Since last Monday, we've had SEVEN. That's why I'm writing in our notebook. This book is supposed to be a diary of our baby-sitting jobs, so each of us can write up our problems and experiences for the other club members to read. But the Baby-sitters Agency is the biggest problem we've ever had, and I plan to keep track of it in our notebook.

We better do something fast.

-Kristy

Chapter 5

AFTER SCHOOL THE NEXT DAY, THE FOUR OF US WALKED HOME TOGETHER.

BALLOONS! WHY DIDN'T **WE** THINK OF BALLOONS?!

YEAH, IT'S TOO BAD.

I KNOW.

YOU GUYS WANT TO COME OVER FOR A WHILE?

GOTTA WORK ON MY OIL PAINTING.

AND I HAVE TO BAKE CRANBERRY BREAD FOR THANKSGIVING DINNER.

I'LL COME OVER, KRISTY.

YEAH, **YOU** JUST WANNA SEE MY BROTHER SAM. . . .

HUH, THE DOOR'S OPEN. . . . WEIRD.

I HOPE MY LITTLE BROTHER DIDN'T GET HOME FIRST. . . . DAVID MICHAEL??

THE BABY'S HERE.

AND YOU WANTED A BOY INSTEAD OF A GIRL, RIGHT?

I DUNNO.

EVERY-THING'S CHANGING, HUH?

UH-HUH . . .

KRISTY CAN'T BABY-SIT ME ANYMORE.

WAIT A MINUTE, JAMIE . . . WHAT DO YOU MEAN??

MOMMY CALLED A GIRL AND SAID, "WE NEED AN OLDER SITTER FOR THE NEW BABY."

WAS THE GIRL NAMED LIZ LEWIS?

49

Chapter 6

TUESDAY MORNING...

...BUT ISN'T IT POSSIBLE JAMIE WAS MISTAKEN? HE'S ONLY THREE. WE DON'T KNOW FOR SURE THAT IT WAS LIZ LEWIS.

YEAH!

I GUESS IT MAKES SENSE THE NEWTONS WOULD WANT SOMEONE OLDER THAN 12 TO WATCH A NEW BABY...

BUT... BUT...

WHAT'S THIS?

LOOK AT THIS. "WANT TO EARN FAST MONEY THE EASY WAY? JOIN THE BABY-SITTERS AGENCY. WE DO THE HARDEST PART--LET THE AGENCY FIND JOBS **FOR** YOU!!"

52

53

Chapter 7

THANKSGIVING WAS ACTUALLY KIND OF FUN.

IT EVEN SNOWED A LITTLE.

IT WAS THE DAY **AFTER** THANKSGIVING THAT MY PARENTS DECIDED TO HIT ME WITH THE NEWS:

SHOULD WE TELL HER NOW, HONEY?

TELL ME **WHAT?!**

WE AREN'T **MOVING** AGAIN, ARE WE?!

HEAVENS, NO.

WE'VE SCHEDULED YOUR TESTS WITH THE NEW DOCTOR, BUT THEY'LL BE A LITTLE LATER IN THE MONTH THAN WE THOUGHT....

NEAR CHRISTMAS?!

WE'LL LEAVE FOR NEW YORK ON FRIDAY, THE TWELFTH, AND PROBABLY RETURN ON WEDNESDAY, THE SEVENTEENTH.

THAT'S **FIVE** DAYS!! YOU SAID WE'D ONLY BE GONE FOR THREE!!

I KNEW IT, I KNEW IT.

NOW, DON'T WORRY...

DR. BARNES ISN'T GOING TO HARM YOU, FROM WHAT I'VE HEARD. HE WON'T TOUCH YOUR INSULIN LEVELS.

BUT WHAT HE PROBABLY **WILL** DO...

...IS RECOMMEND ALL SORTS OF EXPENSIVE PROGRAMS AND THERAPIES.

THERAPIES? LIKE WHAT?

OH, EVERYTHING. SENDING YOU TO A PSYCHIATRIST... EXERCISE PROGRAMS... RECREATIONAL THERAPY...

HE MAY EVEN RECOMMEND THAT YOU CHANGE SCHOOLS, SO YOU CAN GET INDIVIDUALIZED INSTRUCTION.

ERK!

CHANGE SCHOOLS?! NO!!

IT MADE ME THINK OF LAINE, AND WHAT GOOD FRIENDS WE USED TO BE.

SO C'MON, STACE, LET'S DO SOMETHING!

WHAT DO YOU WANT TO DO?

LET'S GO GET ICE CREAM!

YEAH!

OKAY, YOU GIRLS CAN GO BY YOURSELVES, BUT ONLY IF YOU **PROMISE** TO GO AND THEN COME RIGHT BACK.

WE PROMISE!

STACEY, **LOOK!**

Chapter 8

KRISTY HAD A SURPRISE FOR US ON MONDAY MORNING WHEN WE GOT BACK TO SCHOOL.

YOU HAVE **GOT** TO BE KIDDING US!

WHAT?

OH, KRISTY, ARE YOU SERIOUS?!

COME ON, YOU GUYS! PUT THEM ON.

Join the BEST CLUB AROUND!

Join the BEST CLUB AROUND!

The BABY-SITTERS CLUB

UM, GUYS?...

SCHOOL BUS

VROOooMm...

Join the BEST CLUB AROUND!

Join t BEST CLU ARO

Join the BEST CLUB

LATER . . .

WHAT ARE **YOU** SO HAPPY ABOUT, KRISTY? NOBODY WANTS TO JOIN OUR CLUB!

YEAH . . .

I GOT TWO NEW MEMBERS. AND THEY'RE BOTH EIGHTH GRADERS.

REALLY?!

WHAT ARE THEIR NAMES?

JANET GATES AND LESLIE HOWARD.

. . . I THOUGHT THEY WERE FRIENDS OF LIZ'S?

NOT ANYMORE! THEY WERE PART OF THE AGENCY, BUT THEY DROPPED OUT. THEY DIDN'T LIKE IT.

GOSH.

AND THEY'RE COMING TO OUR NEXT MEETING!

CRUNCH CRUNCH

BUT . . . SOMETHING'S WRONG ABOUT THIS. SOMETHING . . . YES, I KNOW WHAT IT IS.

REMEMBER WHEN WE WERE FIRST STARTING THE CLUB, WE ASKED STACEY ALL SORTS OF QUESTIONS ABOUT THE BABY-SITTING SHE DID IN NEW YORK? WE DIDN'T KNOW HER, BUT WE KNEW THAT WE WANTED A CLUB OF GOOD BABY-SITTERS.

AND WE SAW RIGHT AWAY THAT STACEY WAS A GREAT SITTER... BUT DO YOU KNOW **ANYTHING** ABOUT JANET AND LESLIE, KRISTY?

WELL, NO...

AND YOU'VE ALREADY TOLD THEM THEY CAN BE MEMBERS?

YES...

THAT **DOES** SEEM RISKY.

WELL, IT'S TOO LATE NOW. WE'LL JUST HAVE TO TAKE OUR CHANCES.

ANYWAY... IF THE AGENCY IS AS HORRIBLE AS JANET AND LESLIE SAY, MAYBE IT WON'T LAST LONG.

I WONDER IF WE COULD MAKE IT RING IF WE ALL CONCENTRATED ON IT?

SIGH.

Chapter 9

THE NEXT AFTERNOON . . .

GIRLS! HELLO THERE! OH, I'M SO GLAD TO SEE YOU.

HI-HI!

HI, MRS. NEWTON!

COME IN, COME IN. JAMIE HAS MISSED YOU, AND I'M DYING FOR YOU TO MEET LUCY!

MOMMY? ARE ANY OF THOSE PRESENTS FOR ME?

JAMIE . . . IT'S NOT POLITE TO ASK.

YOU'RE IN LUCK, JAMIE . . . FOUR OF THESE PRESENTS ARE FOR YOU.

FOUR!!

I'M SORRY . . . IT'S BEEN A DIFFICULT WEEK. JAMIE HAS BEEN A BIT J-E-A-L-O-U-S. . . . LUCY HAS GOTTEN A LOT OF P-R-E-S-E-N-T-S.

LET'S GO PEEK AT THE BABY BEFORE I OPEN THE REST OF THE GIFTS YOU BROUGHT.

I WISH SHE WERE AWAKE SO YOU COULD HOLD HER, BUT SHE'S STILL NAPPING.

GASP!

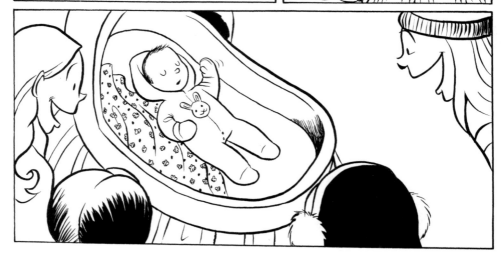

SHE'S SO CUTE!

SHE'S SO TINY!

... MRS. NEWTON? COULD I ASK YOU SOMETHING?

I'M NOT SURE HOW TO SAY THIS, BUT ... JAMIE TOLD STACEY THAT WE WOULDN'T BE BABY-SITTING FOR HIM ANYMORE. HE ... HE HEARD YOU ON THE PHONE WITH LIZ LEWIS FROM THE BABY-SITTERS AGENCY. IS ... CAN WE STILL ... UM ...

I GUESS I SHOULD HAVE TOLD YOU. . . . YOU'LL ALWAYS BE OUR **FAVORITE** SITTERS. . . .

IT'S JUST THAT AN INFANT IS SO DELICATE AND FRAGILE, AND NEEDS EXTRA-SPECIAL CARE.

BUT WE'RE RESPONSIBLE!

I KNOW YOU ARE, BUT FOR THE NEXT FEW MONTHS, I'LL SIMPLY FEEL MORE COMFORTABLE LEAVING LUCY WITH AN OLDER SITTER.

. . . OKAY.

THE TIMES I TAKE LUCY WITH ME AND THERE'S JUST JAMIE TO SIT FOR, I'LL BE GLAD TO CALL THE BABY-SITTERS CLUB.

'BYE, KRISTY!

AND WHEN LUCY IS OLDER, I HOPE YOU'LL BE MY REGULAR SITTERS AGAIN!

SURE!

DEFINITELY.

OF COURSE.

YEAH.

. . . WE'RE DOOMED.

HOW OLD **ARE** YOU?

Snap
Snap
Chew

FOURTEEN.

I'M THIRTEEN.

RINNG

THE PHONE! OH MY GOSH! HELLO, BABY-SITTERS CLUB!

IT'S A NEW CLIENT--THE KELLYS. DO YOU WANT THE JOB, LESLIE?

WHY NOT.

RINNNNNG!!!

DO ONE OF YOU GUYS WANT TO ANSWER THAT?

... NOT REALLY.

GOOD AFTERNOON, BABY-SITTERS CLUB. . . . SURE! OKAY, WE'LL CALL YOU RIGHT BACK.

ANOTHER NEW CLIENT!! WOW. MRS. JAYDELL. SHE'S GOT TWO LITTLE KIDS. IT'S FOR SATURDAY NIGHT.... JANET, DO YOU WANT TO TAKE THIS ONE?

...HUH? OH, I GUESS.

HELLO, MRS. JAYDELL?...

THIS IS GOOD... THIS IS REALLY GOOD.

I'M SO RELIEVED!

IT SEEMED THE BABY-SITTERS CLUB WAS BACK ON TRACK.

RING!

WE HAD NO IDEA HOW WRONG WE WERE.

Monday, December 8

Today. Kristy, Stacey + Mary Anne all arived early for our baby-sitters club meeting. We were all realy excited to find out how Janet and Leslie's siting jobs had gone on ~~Sau~~ Saturday.

When it was 5:30 we kept expecting the doorbell to ring any seconde. But it didnt. Soon it was 5:50. Where were they. Krist was getting worried. ~~Hand~~ Write this down in our notebook, somebody, she said. Somethings wrong.

* Claudia *

Chapter 10

OUR NEXT MEETING WAS THE FOLLOWING MONDAY.

BABY-SITTERS CLUB. OH, HI, MRS. MARSHALL! SURE!

CAN SOMEONE WATCH NINA AND ELEANOR ON WEDNESDAY AFTERNOON?

I'LL CHECK.

HEY...

...IT'S AFTER 5:30. SHOULDN'T JANET AND LESLIE BE HERE BY NOW??

HMM, YEAH...

RING!

BABY-SITTERS CLUB... MRS. NEWTON!! HI!

FOR JUST JAMIE? OF COURSE!

RING!

BABY-SI-- OH, HI, WATSON! YEAH, I'D LOVE TO SIT FOR KAREN AND ANDREW! LET ME SEE IF I'M FREE THEN...

5:50

UM... YOU GUYS?

THEY COULD HAVE AT LEAST CALLED TO SAY THEY WEREN'T GOING TO MAKE TODAY'S MEETING . . .

I SAW JANET IN SCHOOL TODAY, AND SHE DIDN'T SAY ANYTHING ABOUT NOT COMING.

WELL, I'LL CALL THEM TO SEE IF--

RING!

HELLO, BABY-SITTERS CLUB. YES, THIS IS KRISTY THOMAS, CLUB PRESIDENT . . . OH, HELLO, MR. KELLY . . .

SHE **DIDN'T?!**

I'M SO SORRY. I DIDN'T KNOW. WELL, SHE ISN'T HERE RIGHT NOW. . . . I FEEL TERRIBLE.

click

LESLIE NEVER SHOWED UP FOR HER JOB AT THE KELLYS ON SATURDAY.

WHAT?! WHY DIDN'T THE KELLYS CALL US ON SATURDAY?

SIMPLE! LESLIE SHOWED THEM WE WEREN'T TRUSTWORTHY! MR. KELLY WAS ONLY CALLING NOW TO MAKE SURE WE KNEW ABOUT IT . . . BUT I HAVE A FEELING THE KELLYS WON'T BE CALLING THE BABY-SITTERS CLUB AGAIN.

RING!

HELLO, BABY-SITTERS CLUB. YES? . . . OH, NO, YOU'RE **KIDDING.**

IT'S MRS. JAYDELL.

MRS. JAYDELL? DID JANET NOT SHOW UP FOR HER JOB?

GRAB

NO, WE HAD NO IDEA. I'M SORRY YOU MISSED THE COCKTAIL PARTY . . . YES . . . I UNDERSTAND.

CLICK!

AAAAAAAAAHH!!

81

THE NEXT DAY . . .

WE ARE GOING TO TEACH THOSE TRAITORS A **LESSON.**

YOU'RE SURE THEY FLAKED OUT ON THEIR JOBS ON PURPOSE??

POSITIVE.

THEIR HOMEROOMS ARE BOTH IN THIS HALL. SO WE'LL WAIT FOR THEM HERE.

. . . I SEE THEM! AND THEY'RE WITH . . .

LIZ AND MICHELLE WILL JUST HAVE TO WORK A LITTLE HARDER TO BE THE BEST SITTING AGENCY IN TOWN. LATER!

I'M SO EMBARRASSED! I SHOULD HAVE CHECKED ON THEM FIRST.

IT'S OKAY, KRISTY.

WE'LL JUST HAVE TO KEEP GOING. THE FOUR OF US. SO WHAT IF WE'RE ONLY TWELVE? SO WHAT IF WE CAN'T STAY OUT LATE?

YEAH!

I THINK **WE'RE** THE BETTER BABY-SITTING SERVICE.... WE JUST HAVE TO THINK OF A WAY TO PROVE IT!

Wednesday, December 10th

Earlier this afternoon, I baby-sat for Jamie while Mrs. Newton took Lucy to a doctor's appointment. Something was bothering him. He moped around as if he'd lost his best friend. He greeted me cheerfully enough when I arrived, but as soon as Mrs. Newton carried a bundled-up Lucy out the back door, his face fell....

                              Mary Anne

Chapter 11

ONE OF YOUR SITTERS DID THAT?!

YES.

WITH A CIGARETTE.

GOSH... ANYTHING ELSE?

SOMETIMES THEY TALK ON THE PHONE. THEY TALK LONGER THAN MOMMY AND DADDY DO.... MARY ANNE?

YES?

MARY ANNE'S

WHAT'S A BOYFRIEND?

IT'S...UM...IT'S A FRIEND WHO'S A BOY.

AM I YOUR BOYFRIEND?

NOT EXACTLY. LISTEN, JAMIE... WHO BABY-SITS FOR YOU NOW? DO YOU KNOW THEIR NAMES?

HI, STACEY. I'M GLAD YOU'RE HERE. . . . CHARLOTTE HAS BEEN IN A FUNNY MOOD LATELY.

SHE SAYS SHE FEELS FINE, BUT SHE'S BEEN VERY OUT OF SORTS. I'VE ARRANGED A CONFERENCE WITH HER TEACHER.

BUT I JUST WANTED YOU TO KNOW.

MR. JOHANSSEN IS WORKING LATE TONIGHT, AND I HAVE A P.T.A. MEETING. WE'LL BOTH BE BACK BEFORE 9:00.

OKAY.

WHEN YOU COME HOME, COULD I TALK TO YOU? WE'RE LEAVING FOR NEW YORK ON SATURDAY, AND I HAVE AN IDEA.

CERTAINLY.

SEE YOU LATER, SWEETIE.

MMM.

SO! DO YOU NEED ANY HELP WITH YOUR HOMEWORK, CHARLOTTE?

NO, IT'S EASY.

93

HEY, CHAR . . . I INVITED YOU TO JAMIE NEWTON'S BIG BROTHER PARTY DIDN'T I? I WASN'T SITTING FOR YOU THEN.

SNIFF YEAH . . .

AND WHAT DO MICHELLE AND LESLIE AND CATHY DO WHEN THEY BABY-SIT FOR YOU?

WATCH TV. TALK ON THE PHONE. ONCE LESLIE BROUGHT HER BOYFRIEND OVER.

WHAT DO I DO WHEN I BABY-SIT?

WELL, YOU BRING THE KID-KIT. WE READ STORIES, AND TAKE WALKS, AND PLAY GAMES. . . .

THAT'S BEING A FRIEND, ISN'T IT?

...YES!! I'M SORRY, STACEY. I'M SORRY I WAS ANGRY.

DO YOU WANT TO TALK TO ME ABOUT THOSE KIDS AT YOUR SCHOOL? THE ONES WHO WERE TEASING YOU?

NO.

WELL, IF YOU EVER NEED TO TALK ABOUT IT, YOU CAN ALWAYS TALK TO ME!

LATER...

SO, STACEY, WHAT DID YOU WANT TO TALK TO ME ABOUT?

WELL, I FIGURE I'LL LET MOM AND DAD TAKE ME TO THEIR "DOCTOR" ON SATURDAY...

BUT I ALSO WANT TO TELL THEM I'VE BEEN RESEARCHING DIABETES ON MY OWN, AND TELL THEM ABOUT A DOCTOR **I'VE** CHOSEN WHO I WANT TO SEE. WHICH IS WHERE YOU COME IN.

I WAS HOPING YOU COULD RECOMMEND SOMEONE SENSIBLE... AND PREFERABLY, SOMEONE WITH A FANCY OFFICE AND LOTS OF DIPLOMAS.

WELL, I WAS ACTUALLY ABOUT TO **GIVE** YOU A RECOMMENDATION. WE MUST'VE BEEN THINKING ALONG THE SAME LINES.

IF I PULL A FEW STRINGS, I SHOULD BE ABLE TO GET YOU AN APPOINTMENT FOR SATURDAY.

OH, THANK YOU!!!

BUT I'D RATHER EXPLAIN THINGS TO YOUR PARENTS.

OH, NO, PLEASE DON'T!! IT HAS TO BE A SURPRISE... OTHERWISE IT'LL **NEVER** WORK.

WELL . . . HOW ABOUT IF I WRITE A LETTER TO YOUR PARENTS? YOU CAN GIVE IT TO THEM OVER THE WEEKEND . . . BEFORE YOU SEE THE DOCTOR.

. . . ALL RIGHT. I GUESS THAT'LL WORK.

THANKS, DR. JOHANSSEN!

SLAM!

104

I DID WHAT YOU SAID!!

COULD WE TALK TO YOU ALONE?

O--OF COURSE... IS SOMETHING WRONG?

I GUESS WE SHOULD BEGIN WITH WHAT HAPPENED THIS AFTERNOON.

WE WERE WALKING HOME FROM SCHOOL, AND WE SAW JAMIE PLAYING OUTSIDE.

BY HIMSELF.

IN THE STREET.

WITH NO HAT OR MITTENS.

HE TOLD US CATHY MORRIS WAS BABY-SITTING FOR HIM, BUT SHE WAS NOWHERE TO BE SEEN... WE DON'T THINK SHE KNEW WHERE JAMIE WAS.

WE FELT YOU REALLY OUGHT TO KNOW.

!

107

Chapter 13

OH, LIKE, LOOK WHO IT IS. THE BABY CLUB.

LIKE, HA HA.

WHAT, SO YOUR LITTLE CLUB FAILED, AND NOW YOU WANT TO COME WORK FOR US?

NO WAY. WE'RE HERE TO TALK ABOUT AN IMPORTANT BUSINESS MATTER.

AND WHAT IS SO IMPORTANT?

YESTERDAY CATHY MORRIS WAS SITTING FOR A THREE-YEAR-OLD, AND SHE LET HIM GO OUTDOORS BY HIMSELF.

SO?

110

OKAY, SO YOU PROVED IT. NOW GO AWAY AND LEAVE US ALONE.

THAT AFTERNOON...

SO, WHO'RE WE STAYING WITH THIS TIME--AUNT BEV AND UNCLE LOU, OR AUNTIE CARLA AND UNCLE ERIC?

WE'RE NOT STAYING WITH EITHER OF THEM.

GASP YOU MEAN WE'RE STAYING IN A HOTEL?!

NO...

WE'RE STAYING WITH THE CUMMINGSES. YOU CAN SEE LAINE AGAIN!

WHAT?! THE CUMMINGSES??

DO THEY KNOW WHAT'S WRONG WITH ME, THEN? HAVE YOU FINALLY TOLD THEM ABOUT MY DIABETES?

YES, WE FINALLY TOLD THEM. LAINE KNOWS, TOO.

HOW COULD YOU DO THIS TO ME?! YOU KNOW LAINE HATES ME. AND I HATE HER.

OH, STACEY. THAT WAS MONTHS AGO. I'M SURE YOU AND LAINE ARE OVER THAT FIGHT!

HI.

HMPH!

I JUST WANT YOU TO KNOW THAT I'M NOT ANY HAPPIER ABOUT THIS THAN YOU ARE. I WANTED TO STAY IN A HOTEL.

STACEY--

SLAM!

THAT NIGHT, I NOTICED LAINE WATCHING ME VERY CAREFULLY.

BUT THERE WASN'T MUCH FOR HER TO SEE.

I DON'T KNOW WHAT SHE WAS EXPECTING. NOBODY GAVE ME ANY SPECIAL ATTENTION, FOOD, OR FAVORS.

114

THE NEXT MORNING...

MR. AND MRS. MCGILL? DR. BARNES WILL MEET WITH YOU IN A FEW MINUTES. STACEY, PLEASE COME WITH ME.

?!

WE'LL SEE YOU AGAIN SOON, STACEY.

MOM? DAD?

CAN WE GO NEXT DOOR AND GET SOMETHING TO DRINK?

YES, GOOD IDEA.

. . . AND THEN SHE MADE ME TAKE WHAT I **THINK** WAS AN I.Q. TEST. AND I HAVEN'T EVEN SEEN DR. BARNES YET! WHAT'S HE LIKE?

SANDWIC
Brie, Apple
Cheddar, Ha
Fresh Moz
Gruyère C
Roast Bee
Turkey, Av

HE'S . . . WELL . . .

LISTEN, MOM, DAD . . . I'VE BEEN THINKING. YOU GUYS WERE RIGHT. IT'S IMPORTANT TO LEARN ABOUT DIABETES, AND HOW TO LIVE WITH IT.

I'VE BEEN LOOKING INTO IT MYSELF.

YOU HAVE? GOOD FOR YOU.

YEAH, AND I . . . I HEARD ABOUT THIS DOCTOR, DR. GRAHAM.

HE'S A BIG AUTHORITY ON CHILDHOOD DISEASES, ESPECIALLY DIABETES.

THE THING IS, I HAVE AN APPOINTMENT WITH HIM TODAY. IT'S SORT OF A SURPRISE.

THIS IS FROM CHARLOTTE'S MOTHER, DR. JOHANSSEN. I THINK YOU'D BETTER READ IT NOW.

WHAT? HONEY, I--

JUST **READ** IT.

THE LETTER EXPLAINED THAT I HAD GONE TO DR. JOHANSSEN CONFIDENTIALLY, WHICH WAS WHY SHE HADN'T CONTACTED MY PARENTS PERSONALLY.

IT ALSO PRAISED DR. GRAHAM'S WORK, AND APOLOGIZED TO MOM AND DAD FOR ANY INCONVENIENCE.

STACEY, I'M NOT QUITE SURE WHAT TO THINK OF ALL THIS.

I THOUGHT YOU'D BE PLEASED.

WE ARE, WE JUST... WE DON'T KNOW ANYTHING ABOUT HIM. WE DON'T KNOW HOW EXPENSIVE HE IS, OR...

I WISH YOU'D DISCUSSED THIS WITH US BEFORE YOU MADE AN APPOINTMENT.

YOU MAKE APPOINTMENTS FOR ME WITHOUT ASKING **ME** FIRST.

TRUE . . .

DR. GRAHAM . . . HIS NAME SOUNDS FAMILIAR.

YES.

HE'S SUPPOSED TO BE EXCELLENT, BUT VERY BUSY AND ALMOST IMPOSSIBLE TO SEE. YOU WERE LUCKY TO GET AN APPOINTMENT.

WELL, MY APPOINTMENT'S IN 15 MINUTES. . . . WE'D BETTER GET GOING IF WE WANT TO MAKE IT.

HELLO, YOU MUST BE STACEY. I'M DR. PHILIP GRAHAM.

HI!

WE'RE SORRY SHE SET UP THE APPOINTMENT WITHOUT . . .

IT'S NO PROBLEM. WON'T YOU HAVE A SEAT?

I'M NOT GOING TO EXAMINE STACEY TODAY. . . I JUST WANT TO ASK SOME QUESTIONS.

SOME QUESTIONS! HE ASKED A BILLION. ABOUT MY BIRTH, MY HEALTH BEFORE THE DIABETES WAS DISCOVERED, MY NEW SCHOOL, MY FRIENDS.

WE TALKED FOREVER, AND HE EVEN MADE MY PARENTS FEEL COMFORTABLE.

WELL . . . YOU MUST BE VERY PROUD OF YOUR DAUGHTER.

OH, YES, ABSOLUTELY.

FROM WHAT YOU'VE TOLD ME, STACEY WAS A VERY SICK YOUNG LADY, BUT SHE'S MADE EXCELLENT PROGRESS WITH HER TREATMENT.

I CAN ONLY SEE ONE PROBLEM.

WHAT'S THAT??

ALTHOUGH STACEY HAS TAKEN THE MOVE TO CONNECTICUT IN STRIDE, SHE SEEMS TO FEEL QUITE UNSETTLED ABOUT HER DISEASE.

SHE WANTS TO BE ABLE TO HAVE SOME CONTROL OVER IT, BUT SHE'S A LITTLE AFRAID OF IT. IS THAT RIGHT?

WELL . . .

I GUESS. EVERY TIME I THINK I UNDERSTAND IT, WE SEE SOME **OTHER** DOCTOR WHO SAYS SOMETHING DIFFERENT.

DR. JOHANSSEN SAID SHE THINKS DR. BARNES MIGHT MAKE ME GO TO A PSYCHIATRIST, OR EVEN CHANGE SCHOOLS.

BUT I DON'T **WANT** TO CHANGE SCHOOLS! I DON'T WANT TO SEE ANY MORE DOCTORS!

I MUST ADMIT. . . WE **WERE** A BIT PERPLEXED BY MANY OF THE TESTS DR. BARNES WAS PLANNING TO GIVE STACEY ON MONDAY AND TUESDAY.

WHAT DO **YOU** THINK OF DR. BARNES' CLINIC?

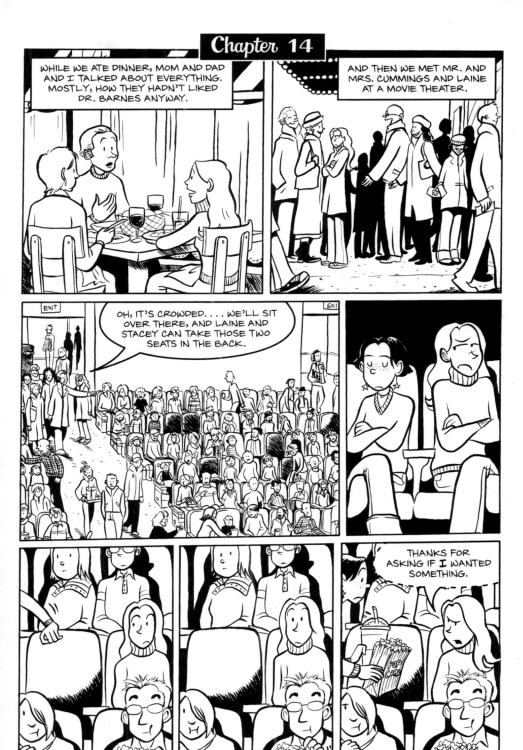

Chapter 14

WHILE WE ATE DINNER, MOM AND DAD AND I TALKED ABOUT EVERYTHING. MOSTLY, HOW THEY HADN'T LIKED DR. BARNES ANYWAY.

AND THEN WE MET MR. AND MRS. CUMMINGS AND LAINE AT A MOVIE THEATER.

OH, IT'S CROWDED. . . . WE'LL SIT OVER THERE, AND LAINE AND STACEY CAN TAKE THOSE TWO SEATS IN THE BACK.

THANKS FOR ASKING IF **I** WANTED SOMETHING.

YOU CAN'T EAT ANY OF THIS STUFF ANYWAY.

I CAN EAT POPCORN. I CAN DRINK DIET SODA.

POP CORN

FREE2

WELL, I DIDN'T KNOW!

IF YOU EVER BOTHERED TO SPEAK TO ME, YOU'D...

SHHH!!

YOU DON'T TALK TO ME EITHER. YOU NEVER EVEN TOLD ME THE TRUTH ABOUT YOUR...YOUR SICKNESS.

WHY WOULD I WANT TO TALK TO SOMEONE WHO TURNS ALL MY FRIENDS AGAINST....

SHHH!!

POP CORN

EXCUSE ME, LAINE. I'D LIKE TO GET MYSELF A SNACK.

A SMALL DIET COKE AND A SMALL POPCORN, NO BUTTER, PLEASE.

THAT'LL BE $9.25.

Beep Beep

YEAH.

I'M SORRY, TOO. . . . I GUESS I SHOULD HAVE TOLD YOU WHAT WAS WRONG WITH ME.

BUT MOM AND DAD WEREN'T TELLING ANYONE EXCEPT FAMILY, SO I . . . HOW COME YOU STOPPED BEING MY FRIEND?

. . . I DON'T KNOW.

I MEAN, ACTUALLY, I THINK I **DO** KNOW--THIS IS GOING TO SOUND RIDICULOUS, BUT I WAS JEALOUS.

WHAT?! JEALOUS OF ME? YOU **WANTED** TO BE SICK?!

OF COURSE NOT. BUT, YOU WERE GETTING SO MUCH ATTENTION FROM THE TEACHERS. . . .

EVERYONE WAS ALWAYS ASKING YOU HOW YOU FELT, AND GIVING YOU EXTENSIONS ON OUR ASSIGNMENTS. . . .

AND YOU GOT TO MISS A TON OF SCHOOL.

LAINE, I MISSED SO MUCH I NEARLY HAD TO **REPEAT** SIXTH GRADE.

ARE YOU SERIOUS? WOW. I DIDN'T KNOW THAT. WELL, ANYWAY, REMEMBER BOBBY REEDER?

HE THOUGHT YOU WERE CONTAGIOUS, AND FOR SOME REASON, I BELIEVED HIM. SINCE I WAS YOUR BEST FRIEND, I WAS POSITIVE I WAS GOING TO GET "IT," WHATEVER IT WAS.

OH.

WHEN MY PARENTS FOUND OUT ABOUT OUR FIGHT, THEY WERE PRETTY MAD AT ME. WE TALKED ABOUT IT, BUT I DIDN'T KNOW HOW TO APOLOGIZE TO YOU.

THAT'S WHY I NEVER WROTE TO YOU AFTER YOU MOVED AWAY.

WELL, I **WAS** PRETTY MAD. . .

BUT I GUESS IT WOULD'VE HELPED IF I'D TOLD YOU THE TRUTH.

Poke!

YOU KNOW, EVERY NOW AND THEN, I WONDER ABOUT THE PEOPLE HERE.

LIKE WHO?

WELL, I REMEMBER DEIRDRE DUNLOP USED TO BRAG SHE'D BE THE FIRST IN OUR CLASS TO OUTGROW HER TRAINING BRA. . . . DID SHE?

SNORT!

YES! AND THE **DAY** SHE CAME IN WEARING HER NEW BRA, LOWELL JOHNSTON ASKED HER FOR A DATE!

NO WAY!

POP CORN

POP CORN

STACEY, LOOK!

THE MOVIE'S OVER?! WOW! WE MISSED THE WHOLE THING!

YEAH!

BUT IT WAS WORTH IT!

LAINE AND I REALIZED WE HAD A LOT OF CATCHING UP TO DO, SO WE MADE THE MOST OF THE WEEKEND.

AND WHEN WE WENT TO SLEEP ON SUNDAY NIGHT, I FELT LIKE A HUGE WEIGHT HAD BEEN LIFTED FROM MY CHEST.

'NIGHT, LAINE.

'NIGHT, STACE.

WELL, TWO, ACTUALLY...

HELLO, DR. BARNES... YES, I'M SORRY, BUT WE'VE DECIDED TO CANCEL THE REST OF STACEY'S TESTS THIS WEEK.

AND THEN WE WERE **HOME!!**

133

STACEY, YOU **KNOW** YOU'RE SUPPOSED TO OFFER EVERY JOB THAT COMES ALONG TO ALL THE MEMBERS OF THE CLUB.

I'M SORRY....
I JUST FORGOT.
I WAS SO EXCITED.

...I KNOW.

IT'S OKAY, I'D BE PRETTY EXCITED ABOUT SITTING FOR LUCY, TOO. BESIDES... I'VE BROKEN THAT RULE OFTEN ENOUGH MYSELF.

STACEY!

Chapter 15

136

...LIZ AND MICHELLE WERE HANDING OUT FLIERS FOR A **NEW** BUSINESS!!

MAKEOVERS, INC.

$5 to sign up!!!

MAKEOVERS, INC.?

YOU PAY THEM $5.00, AND THEY SHOW YOU HOW TO PUT ON MAKEUP, FIGURE OUT THE BEST WAY FOR YOU TO FIX YOUR HAIR...

OH, NO THANKS.

MAKEOVERS INC.

NOBODY SEEMED INTERESTED IN THEIR NEW SCHEME!

HA HA!

OH, AND GUESS WHAT-- CHARLOTTE JOHANSSEN, THE LITTLE GIRL WHO WAS HAVING TROUBLE WITH HER CLASSMATES...

YEAH?

HER TEACHER IS GOING TO SKIP HER INTO **THIRD** GRADE! THE WORK IN SECOND GRADE IS TOO EASY FOR HER.

THAT'S WHY THE OTHER KIDS WERE TEASING HER.

CHARLOTTE'S REALLY EXCITED ABOUT STARTING FRESH IN THE NEW YEAR.

AWW. THAT'S GOOD... I REALLY WISH I COULD MEET HER--I'D LOVE TO MEET **ALL** YOUR FRIENDS THERE, STACEY.

WELL, YOU SHOULD COME VISIT ME IN STONEYBROOK!

REALLY??

YES! AND WHEN YOU DO...

This book is for my old pal, Claudia Werner

A. M. M.

Very big thanks to Marion Vitus, Adam Girardet,
Duane Ballanger, Lisa Jonté, Arthur Levine, KC Witherall,
and Hope Larson. As always, a huge thank you to my
family, my friends, and especially, Dave.

R. T.

Text © 2006 by Ann M. Martin.
Art © 2006 by Raina Telgemeier.

All rights reserved. Published by Graphix, an imprint of Scholastic Inc.,
Publishers since 1920. SCHOLASTIC, GRAPHIX, THE BABY-SITTERS
CLUB, and associated logos are trademarks and/or registered trade-
marks of Scholastic Inc.

No part of this publication may be reproduced, stored in a retrieval
system, or transmitted in any form or by any means, electronic,
mechanical, photocopying, recording, or otherwise, without written
permission of the publisher. For information regarding permission, write
to Scholastic Inc., Attention: Permissions Department, 557 Broadway,
New York, NY 10012.

Library of Congress Cataloging-in-Publication Data is available.
ISBN 0-439-86724-X (hardcover) ISBN 0-439-73936-5 (paperback)

10 9 8 7 6 5 4 3 2 1   06 07 08 09 10

First edition, November 2006
Lettering by John Green
Edited by David Levithan & Janna Morishima
Book design by Kristina Albertson
Creative Director: David Saylor
Printed in the U.S.A.

Harris County Public Library
Houston, Texas